CW00920302

Contents

The Death of a Civil Servant
Civil Servant
and Other Stories

The Death of a
Civil Servant

ONE FINE EVENING, an equally fine administrative clerk, Ivan Dmitrich Chervyakov, was sitting in the second row of the orchestra and watching a performance of *The Chimes of Normandy** through his opera glasses. He watched, and felt that he was at the very height of bliss. But suddenly… (In stories, one often encounters this "But suddenly…" The authors are right: life is so full of surprises!) But suddenly his face wrinkled up, his eyes rolled, his breathing stopped… He lowered the opera glasses, bent forward, and… Kerchoo! He sneezed, as you have seen.

Now, sneezing is not forbidden to anybody anywhere. Muzhiks sneeze, and police chiefs, and sometimes even privy councillors. Everybody sneezes. Chervyakov was not at all embarrassed. He wiped his face with his handkerchief and, like the polite man he was, looked around to see whether he had disturbed anyone with his sneezing. But then he found reason enough to be embarrassed. He noticed that the little old man sitting in front of him, in the first row, was vigorously wiping his bald pate and the back of his neck with his glove, and muttering something. Chervyakov recognized the little old man as Civil Service General Brizzhalov, of the Ministry of Railways.

"I splattered him!" Chervyakov thought. "He's not my boss, but it's still awkward. I'll have to apologize."

He coughed, leant forward in his seat, and whispered into the General's ear, "Pardon me, Your Excellency, for splattering you... It was an accident..."

"No harm done. Forget it."

"Please forgive me! I... I didn't mean to."

"Oh, do sit back! I can't hear what they're saying!"

Chervyakov became flustered. He smiled stupidly, and went back to watching the play. He watched, but he felt no more bliss. Anxiety began to torment him. During intermission he approached Brizzhalov, stalled around until he had conquered his shyness, and then mumbled, "Your Excellency, I splattered you... Forgive me... Honestly... I didn't mean..."

"Oh, leave off it! I'd already forgotten it, but you keep harping away!" said the General, his lower lip twitching with impatience.

"He says he's forgotten, but there's a mean look in his eye," thought Chervyakov, glancing at the General suspiciously. "He doesn't even want to talk about it. I ought to explain to him that I hadn't the slightest intention of... that it was just a law of nature. If I don't, he'll think I intended to spit on him, as the saying goes. He may not think so right now, but he will later..."

When he got home, Chervyakov told his wife about his stupid behaviour. She took the incident too lightly, it seemed to him. She was merely startled; and then, when she found out that Brizzhalov was "somebody else's boss", she relaxed.

"But you should still go and apologize," she said, "or he'll think you don't know how to behave in public."

"But that's just it! I did apologize! But he acted strangely – didn't say one sensible word. Besides, there was no time to talk it over."

The next day Chervyakov put on a new uniform dress coat, got a haircut, and went to Brizzhalov's to explain… As he entered the General's reception room, he saw a whole lot of petitioners, and in their midst the General himself, who had already begun to hear requests. When he had dealt with several petitioners, the General looked up and noticed Chervyakov.

"Last night at the Arcadia Theatre," the clerk began to report, "if Your Excellency will recall,

I sneezed and accidentally splattered you...
Please for—"

"Such stupid trifles! What is this, anyway?"
And the General turned to the next petitioner.
"What can I do for you?"

"He doesn't want to talk about it!" thought
Chervyakov, growing pale. "That means he's
angry... No, I can't leave things like this... I'll
explain to him..."

When the General had concluded his audience with the last petitioner and was headed for
his private chambers, Chervyakov followed him
and mumbled, "Your Excellency! If I dare to
disturb you, Excellency, it is only, I can assure
you, out of a feeling of repentance... What I
did was not done on purpose – please take note
of that."

The General made a face as if about to cry, and waved his hand. "Why, sir, you're simply mocking me!" he said, and vanished behind the door.

"What kind of mockery does he mean?" thought Chervyakov. "I'm not mocking him in the slightest! He may be a general, but he doesn't understand. And if that's the way it is, I won't make any more explanations to that braggart. The devil with him! I'll write him a letter, but I won't try to see him in person. Never again!"

Such were Chervyakov's thoughts as he went home. But he didn't write any letter to the General. He thought and thought, but he couldn't think up a letter. So the next day he had to go in person to explain.

"The reason I came and bothered you yesterday, Your Excellency," he mumbled, when the General looked up at him with questioning eyes, "was not, as you deigned to say, to mock you. I was apologizing because, when I sneezed, I splattered you. I had no idea of mocking you. Would I dare mock you? If people like me started mocking others, there would be no respect for... for persons of—"

"Get out!" barked the General, who had suddenly turned purple and started to tremble.

"W-what, sir?" Chervyakov asked in a whisper, going faint with fright.

"Get out!" repeated the General, stamping his feet.

In Chervyakov's stomach, something broke loose. Seeing nothing and hearing nothing, he

back-pedalled to the door, went out into the
street, and shuffled away… Arriving home like
a sleepwalker, he lay down on the sofa without
taking off his dress coat, and died.

– 1883

A Calculated Marriage

A Novel in Two Parts

Part One

A T THE WIDOW MYMRINA's house, in Five Dogs Lane, a wedding supper is in progress. Twenty-three people are at the table, eight of whom are passing up the food, complaining of feeling "urpy", and nodding their heads drowsily. The candles, the lamps and a twisted chandelier borrowed from a tavern are blazing so brightly that one of the guests sitting at the table, a telegrapher, squints affectedly and keeps bringing up, apropos of nothing, the subject of electrical lighting. He prophesies a great future for this kind of illumination, and for electricity in general; but the others are nonetheless rather disdainful towards what he has to say.

"Electricity…" mutters the nuptial godfather, staring stupidly at his plate. "In my opinion electric lighting is only a swindle! They stick a little piece of coal in there and think they're fooling us! No, friend, if you're going to give me lighting, don't make it a little piece of coal. Give me something substantial, something you can light up, something a man can get hold of! Give me flame – understand? Flame that's natural, not mental!"

"If you'd ever seen an electric battery and what it's made of," says the telegrapher, showing off, "you'd think different."

"I don't even want to see one. It's a swindle… They're bilking us ordinary folks – squeezing the last drop out of us. Oh, we know them and their kind!… But as for you, Mr Young Man – I

don't have the honour of knowing your name –
instead of taking sides with swindlers, you'd do
better to drink up and pour drinks for others."

The bridegroom, Aplombov, a young man
with a long neck and bristly hair, says in a
raspy tenor voice, "I entirely agree with you,
Papa. Why start these intellectual conversa-
tions? Me, I can talk about all kinds of discov-
eries in a scientific way! But that's for another
time, after all. And what is your opinion, *ma
chère*?" the bridegroom asks the bride, sitting
next to him.

Dashenka, the bride, on whose face are in-
scribed all the virtues but one – a capacity for
thinking – flushes, and says, "He wants to show
off his education, and he's always talking about
things a body can't understand no how."

"Praise be to God we've lived all our lives without education, and now, thank the Lord, we're marrying off our third daughter to a decent man," says Dashenka's mother from the other end of the table, signing and turning to the telegrapher. "But if to your way of thinking we act uneducated, why come here? Better you should go visit some of your educated friends!"

Silence descends. The telegrapher is flustered. He had never expected the talk about electricity to take such an unlikely turn. The silence is of a hostile kind. It seems to him a symptom of general displeasure, and he thinks he must justify himself.

"Tatyana Petrovna," he says, "I have always respected your family. And if I mentioned electric lighting, that still doesn't mean I did it out of pride. I'll be glad to drink up… With all my heart I have always hoped Dashenka would get a good husband. In these times, Tatyana Petrovna, a good husband is hard to find. Today everybody is out to get married for material gain – for money."

"You're insinuating!" says the bridegroom, getting red in the face and blinking his eyes.

"I'm not insinuating at all," says the telegrapher, feeling a bit frightened. "I'm not speaking of present company. I just meant… in general… O good Lord! Everybody knows you married for love! The dowry was a mere trifle…"

"No! It was not a mere trifle!" the insulted mother of the bride objects. "Talk away, but watch what you say! Along with the thousand roubles, we're giving three coats, bed linen and all this furniture! Just you try and find a dowry like that anywhere else!"

"But I didn't mean anything… Certainly the furniture is good… I just said that because he was offended, as if I had insinuated—"

"Just make sure you *don't* insinuate!" says the bride's mother. "We've always had a regard for you because of your parents. And we invited you to the wedding, and now you're saying all kinds of insulting things… Besides, if you knew Yegor Fyodorych was marrying for money, why did you keep quiet about it? You should have come to us like one of the family, and said, 'The thing is, he just wants to feather his nest.' As for you, *batyushka*"* – and she turns to the bridegroom, her tearful eyes blinking. "It's a sin! I raised her and reared her the best way I could.

She's been the apple of my eye, this dear little child of mine. And now you... just to feather your nest..."

"And you believed that slander?" says Aplombov, getting up from his side of the table and nervously plucking at his bristly hair. "My most humble thanks! *Merci* for such an opinion! And you, Mr Blinchikov!" He turns to the telegrapher. "For all that you are an acquaintance of mine, I won't allow you to commit such outrages in somebody else's home. Kindly get out!"

"What's that you said?"

"Kindly get out! I want you to be as honourable a man as I am. In a word, kindly get out!"

"Lay off it! That's enough!" The bridegroom's friends try to cool him down. "Is it worth it? Sit down! Lay off it!"

"No! I want to prove he has no real right on his side! It was for love that I entered into the state of matrimony. Why are you still sitting there? I don't understand! Kindly get out!"

"I didn't mean anything… Why, I…" says the bewildered telegrapher, getting up from the table. "I just don't understand… All right, then, I'll go… But first give me back the three roubles you borrowed from me to buy the piqué vest. I'll have one more quick one, and then go. But first pay me what you owe me."

There is prolonged whispering among the bridegroom and his friends. The latter give him three roubles in small change. He indignantly throws it at the telegrapher. And he, after a long search for his uniform cap, bows, and leaves.

Such is the way a harmless discussion of

electricity can sometimes end up. However, the supper is now almost over… Night is falling. The well-bred author curbs his fantasy with a strong bit, and throws a dark veil of mystery over immediate events.

Rosy-fingered Dawn finds Hymen still in Five Dogs Lane. But now the grey morn arrives, and gives the author abundant material for

The Second and Final Part

A GREY MORNING IN AUTUMN. It is not yet eight o'clock, but there is unusual commotion in Five Dogs Lane. Perturbed policemen and doormen are running along the pavements; kitchen maids, chilled to the bone, are crowding about at the gates, with expressions of great bewilderment on their faces... From all the windows, inhabitants look out. And women's heads crane out from the open window of the laundry, with temples and chins squeezed against other temples and chins.

"Either it's snow, or it's... no telling what it is!" voices are saying.

Something white that looks very much like snow is swirling in the air, from the ground to the rooftops. The pavement is white. The street lamps, the roofs, the doormen's benches by the gates, the shoulders and caps of passers-by – all are white.

"What happened?" a laundry woman asks some doormen as they run by.

By way of an answer, they wave their hands and keep running... They themselves don't know what it is. But finally one doorman comes slowly along, gesticulating and talking to himself. Obviously, he has been at the scene of the incident and knows everything. "What happened, dearie?" the laundry women ask him from the window.

"Disgruntlement," he replies, "at Mymrina's house, where they had the wedding yesterday. They cheated the bridegroom. Instead of a thousand, they only gave him nine hundred."

"And what did he do?"

"Blew his top. 'I'll this and I'll that,' says he. Then he ripped up the feather bed in a rage, and shook the eiderdown out the window... Just look how much down there is! Just like snow?"

"They're coming! They're coming!" voices cry out.

The procession is moving away from the widow Mymrina's house. First come two policemen with worried expressions. Behind them strides Aplombov in a knitted woollen overcoat, and a top hat. On his face is written, "I am an honourable man, but I don't let anybody swindle me."

"The law will soon show you what kind of a man I am!" he mutters, turning from time to time to look back.

He is followed by Tatyana Petrovna and Dashenka, both in tears. Bringing up the rear is a doorman carrying a book, who is trailed by a crowd of small boys.

"Why are you crying, young wife?" the laundry women ask Dashenka.

"The eiderdown – such a pity!" her mother

answers for her. "A hundred pounds of it, my dears! And what beautiful down! Hand-picked bit by bit, and not one feather in it?"

The procession rounds the corner, and quiet descends upon Five Dogs Lane. The eiderdown drifts through the air until evening.

– 1884

The Culprit

Ashort, exceedingly skinny little peasant in patched pants and a shirt made of mattress ticking stands before the investigating magistrate. His hairy, pockmarked face and his eyes, almost concealed by thick, overhanging brows, have an expression of grimness. A mop of tangled hair that has not been combed for ages makes him look even grimmer in a spiderish way. He is barefoot.

"Denis Grigoryev!" the magistrate begins. "Come up closer and answer my questions. On the morning of 7th July – that is, this month – the railway watchman Ivan Semyonov Akinfov, while walking the tracks, came upon you, at the

141st milepost, unscrewing a nut by which the rails are fastened to the cross-ties. I have the nut here. It was on your person when he arrested you. Is all that true?"

"Whas'at?"

"Did all this happen just as Akinfov stated?"

"Sure enough."

"Very well. Now, why were you unscrewing the nut?"

"Whas'at?"

"Stop saying 'Whas'at?' and answer the question. Why were you unscrewing the nut?"

"If I didn't need it, I wouldn't've unscrewed it," Denis says in a rasping voice, glancing up at the ceiling.

"What need did you have for it?"

"For the nut? We make sinkers out of 'em."

"Who is 'we'?"

"Us folks… The Klimovo muzhiks, I mean."

"Listen, fellow! Don't try playing dumb with me! Just talk sense. No use making up lies about sinkers."

"I never lied in my whole life, and now you say I'm lying," mutters Denis, blinking his eyes. "Could a man do without a sinker, Your Honour? If you put live bait or a worm on the hook, would it go down to the bottom without a sinker?… Sure, I'm lying!" Denis smiles sarcastically. "What damned good is bait if it floats on the surface? Perch and pike and burbot will always go for a baited hook on the bottom. But if it's floating on top, a bullhead's about the only fish that'll take it, and not much of the time at that… Anyway, we don't have no bullheads in our river... That's a fish likes plenty of room."

"Why are you telling me all this about bullheads?"

"Whas'at? On account of you asked me yourself. Up our way the gentlemen fish that way too. Even a little boy wouldn't try to catch fish without a sinker. 'Course a man with poor wits might go fishing without a sinker. There's no rules for fools..."

"So you are saying you unscrewed this nut in order to make a sinker out of it?"

"What else? Not to play knucklebones* with!"

"But for a sinker you could have used a piece of lead, a bullet... perhaps a nail of some kind."

"You don't just find lead on the road – you have to buy it. And a nail's no good. No, you won't find nothing better than a nut. It's heavy, and it's got a hole in it."

"He's still playing dumb! As though he'd been born yesterday, or had dropped out of the sky! Don't you understand, you num-skull, what this unscrewing can lead to? If the watchman hadn't kept a sharp eye out, the train might have gone off the tracks, and people would have been killed! You would have *killed* people!"

"God forbid, Your Honour! Why kill people? Are we unbaptized, or some kind of crimi-nals? Glory be to God, sir! We've lived all our lives and never once had such a thought – much less kill anybody… Save us, Queen of Heaven, and have mercy on us! What are you saying, sir?"

"And what do you think causes train wrecks? Just unscrew two or three nuts, and you'll have your train wreck!"

Denis laughs sarcastically and squints at the magistrate in disbelief. "Humph! All these years all of us in the village have been unscrewing nuts, and the Lord's protected us. And now you talk about train wrecks and killing people!... If I'd hauled off a rail, say, or laid a log crossways on the tracks, maybe then the train would've gone off 'em... But a nut, pshaw!"

"But the nuts hold the rails to the sleepers! Try to get that through your head!"

"Oh, we understand that... After all, we don't unscrew all of 'em... We leave some... We use our heads... We understand."

Denis yawns and makes the sign of the cross over his mouth.

"Last year a train was derailed here," the magistrate says. "Now it's plain to see why it was."

"Beg pardon?"

"I said it is now plain to see why the train was derailed last year… Now I understand it."

"That's why you're educated – you who protect us – so you can understand… The Lord knew who to give understanding to… Here you've gone and figured out how and what… But the watchman, who's just a muzhik like us without any understanding at all, he grabs a man by the collar and drags him in… A person should figure it out first and then do the dragging. But, as the saying goes, a muzhik's got a muzhik's brains… Your Honour, write down that he hit me in the jaw twice – and in the chest, too."

"When your house was searched, one more nut was found… Where did you unscrew it, and when?"

"You mean the one that was under the little red clothes chest?"

"I don't know where you were keeping it, but they found it. When did you unscrew it?"

"I didn't. Ignashka – that's cross-eyed Se-myon's son – he gave it to me, I'm talking now about the one that was under the clothes chest. But the one in the sledge out in the yard – me and Mitrofan unscrewed that one together."

"What Mitrofan?"

"Mitrofan Petrovich. Didn't you ever hear tell of him? He makes fishnets and sells 'em to

the gentlemen. He needs lots of nuts for that —
figure about ten for a net."

"Listen… Article 1081 of the Penal Code
states that any wilful damage to a railway that
might expose to danger the trains travelling
on said railway, provided the perpetrator was
aware that such damage might cause an accident… Do you understand? 'Was aware'! And
you could not help being aware of what this
unscrewing leads to… is punishable by hard
labour in a prison camp."

"Well, you know best… We're just ignorant
folks… How could we understand?"

"You understand the whole thing! You're
lying, faking!"

"Why should I lie? Just ask in the village, if
you don't believe me… A bleak's the only fish

you can catch without a sinker. A gudgeon, now, that's the worst fish of all. But even a gudgeon won't bite if you don't have a sinker."

"And now tell me about bullheads," the magistrate says with a smile.

"We don't have no bullheads in our river... If we cast our lines without any sinker, right on top of the water with a butterfly for bait, maybe a chub will nibble, but mostly not."

"All right, now. Be quiet."

There is a silence. Denis shifts from one foot to the other, stares at the desk covered with green baize, and blinks his eyes hard, as though he were looking at the sun instead of the cloth. The magistrate writes rapidly.

"Can I go now?" Denis asks, after being quiet for a while.

"No. I must take you into custody and send you to prison."

Denis stops blinking and, raising his shaggy eyebrows, looks doubtfully at the official. "What do you mean, 'prison'? Your Honour! I can't spare the time! I have to go to the fair. And I have to get three roubles from Yegor for lard…"

"Be quiet! Don't bother me!"

"To prison!… If I'd done something, I'd go. But just like that… for no reason at all!… For what? I didn't steal anything – not that I know – and I wasn't fighting. If you're thinking I'm behind in my taxes, Your Honour, don't believe the elder… Ask the permanent member of the board… That elder, he's not a Christian at all…"

"Be quiet!"

"I'm being quiet as it is," Denis mutters. "The elder lied in the assessment – I swear he did! There're three of us brothers: Kuzma Grigoryev, then Yegor Grigoryev, and me – Denis Grigoryev…"

"You're bothering me… Hey, Semyon!" the magistrate shouts. "Take him away!"

"There're three of us brothers," Denis is muttering, as two husky soldiers seize him and take him out of the room. "A brother's not supposed to answer for his brother… Kuzma don't pay, so you, Denis, have to answer for him… Judges! Our master, the late general, he died – God rest his soul! If he hadn't, he'd show you judges what's what!… You should use some brains when you judge people – not do it any which way… Flog a man if you like, but for some reason – when it's right and fair…"

– 1885

The Exclamation Mark

A Christmas Story

ON CHRISTMAS EVE, Yefim Fomich Perekladin, a collegiate secretary, went to bed feeling insulted and even abused. "Get thee behind me, Satan!" he roared at his wife, when she asked why he was so gloomy.

The fact was that he had just returned from a party where many things had been said that were unpleasant and insulting to him. At first the guests had begun talking about the usefulness of education in general. Next they had passed naturally to the educational qualifications of the confraternity of government clerks, making a great many pitying remarks, criticisms and even gibes with respect to the low echelons. And then, as so often happens at social gatherings among Russians, they went from general matters to personalities.

"Take yourself, for example, Yefim Fomich," said one young man, turning to him. "You have a rather good position... But what kind of education do you have?"

"None, sir. But our work doesn't require an education," Perekladin replied meekly. "You have to use correct penmanship, that's all."

"And where did you learn to use correct penmanship?"

"I just got into the habit, sir... In forty years of service you can pick up a knack of a thing. Of course it was hard at first, and I made mistakes. But then I got into the habit, and it went along fine..."

"And how about the punctuation marks?"

"They don't give me any trouble. I put them in correctly."

"Hm," said the young man, somewhat at a loss. "But a habit is by no means the same thing as an education. It's not enough that you put in the punctuation marks correctly – not enough, sir! You must be fully aware of what you're doing when you put them in. Oh, yes, sir! As for your unconscious, reflexive penmanship, it's not worth a tinker's damn! It's mechanical production, and nothing more."

Perekladin remained silent, and even smiled meekly. (The young man was the son of a state councillor, and was himself entitled to the tenth rank.) But now, as he went to bed, he became all anger and indignation.

"For forty years I've served," he thought, "and nobody ever called me a simpleton. But now – is it possible? – what criticisms! 'Unconscious'! 'Irreflexive'! 'Mechanical production'!… Oh, the devil take you! But it just may be that I still understand more than you, even if I didn't go to your universities!"

When he had mentally poured out upon his critic all the curses he knew, and had warmed himself under his blanket, Perekladin began to calm down. "I know… I understand," he thought as he began to grow drowsy. "I don't put in a colon where a semicolon is needed. Therefore, I am fully aware. I understand. Yes, I do… So there, young man!… First you have to live and work a while, then you can judge your elders…"

Perekladin was almost asleep. Before his closed eyes, through a throng of dark, smiling clouds, a fiery comma sped like a meteor. After it came another, and then another. Soon the entire background, extending without bounds in his imagination, was covered with thick clusters of whizzing commas...

"Just take those commas, for example," thought Perekladin, feeling in his limbs the sweet numbness of imminent sleep. "I understand them very well indeed... I can find a place for each one of them, if you want, and... with full awareness, not just any which way... Just test me, and you'll see... Commas are put in various places, both where they are needed and where they are not. The more muddled the document is, the more commas it needs.

Commas are placed before 'which' and 'that'. If the document lists the names of officials, each of them must be set off by a comma... I know!"

The golden commas began to spin around and drifted away. Fiery periods sped in to replace them.

"And a full stop is put at the end of a document... A full stop is also placed where it's necessary to take a long breath and look up at the person who is listening. After all long passages, there must be a full stop, so that the secretary, when he reads it aloud, doesn't drool... In no other places are full stops used."

The commas came skittering back... They mixed in with the full stops, swirled about, and Perekladin saw before him a huge throng of semicolons and colons...

"I know them, too," he thought. "When a comma isn't enough, and a full stop is too much, a semicolon is required. Also, a semicolon is always put before 'but' and 'consequently'... And colons? Colons are used after the words 'decreed' and 'resolved'..."

The semicolons and colons faded. It was now the turn of the question marks. They emerged from the clouds and began to dance the cancan...

"That's a fine thing, indeed – the question mark! But even if there were a thousand of them, I'd find a place for all of them. They are always used when an enquiry must be made, or a question is asked about a document. 'What disposition was made of the sums remaining on hand for such-and-such a year?' Or 'Does not the police department find it possible, with regard to the said Ivanov, to?…' And so on."

The question marks nodded their hook-shaped heads in approval, and then promptly – as though by command – straightened themselves up and became exclamation marks.

"Hm!… That punctuation mark is often used in letters. 'Dear Sir!' or 'Your Excellency – Father and Benefactor!'… But when is it used in documents?"

The exclamation marks stretched themselves even taller and stood there waiting…

"In documents they are used when… er… uh… How is that again? Hm!… Come to think of it, when are they used in documents? Wait… Just let me think… Hm!"

Perekladin opened his eyes and rolled over on his other side. But no sooner had he closed his eyes again, than the exclamation marks reappeared against the dark background.

"The devil take them!... When is it they're supposed to be used?" he thought, trying to drive the uninvited guests out of his imagination. "Is it possible I have forgotten? Either I have forgotten, or... or I never used any of them..."

Perekladin began to review in his memory the contents of all the official documents he had copied in his forty years of service. But no matter how hard he thought, or how he wrinkled his brow, in his whole past he could not find a single exclamation mark.

"Now what do you think of that? I've been writing for forty years, and I've never once used an exclamation mark… Hm… But, damn it all, when are they used?"

From behind the row of fiery exclamation marks, the evilly grinning mug of his young critic appeared… The exclamation marks themselves smiled, and merged into one big exclamation mark.

Perekladin shook his head and opened his eyes. "What the devil!" he thought. "I have to get up for early Mass tomorrow morning, and I can't get that damned foolishness out of my head!… Phooey!… But when is it used? There's habit for you! There's 'getting the knack'! A whole forty years, and not one exclamation mark, eh?"

Perekladin crossed himself and closed his eyes, but immediately opened them again: the big exclamation mark was still standing there against the dark background...

"Confound it, I won't get any sleep at all tonight! Marfusha!" he asked his wife, who often bragged of the fact that she had completed boarding school. "Do you happen to know, *du-shenka*,* when exclamation marks are used in official documents?"

"Of course I know! I didn't study seven years at boarding school for nothing! That punctuation mark is used after salutations, exclamations and expressions of rapture, indignation, joy, wrath and other feelings."

"So that's it," thought Perekladin. "'Rapture, indignation, joy, wrath and other feelings'..."

The collegiate secretary brooded... For forty years he had copied documents – he

— 57 —

had copied thousands and tens of thousands of them – but he couldn't remember one line expressing rapture, indignation or anything of the sort...

"'And other feelings'," he thought. "But are feelings necessary in official documents? Documents can be written by a person with no feelings at all..."

The mug of his young critic once again looked out from behind the fiery exclamation mark and grinned evilly. Perekladin got up and sat on the edge of the bed. His head was aching, and cold sweat came out on his brow... In the corner, the icon lamp glowed affectionately, the furniture had a polished, festive appearance – everything exuded warmth and the presence of a feminine touch. But the poor clerk felt cold and comfortless, as though he were coming down with typhus.

And now the exclamation mark was no longer in his mind's eye but standing right there in front of him in the bedroom near his wife's vanity table, and winking at him in mockery.

"A writing machine! A machine!" the phantom whispered, blowing a draught of cold air at him. "A block of wood with no feelings."

The clerk pulled the blanket over his head; but even under the blanket he could still see the phantom. He buried his face in his wife's shoulder; but it loomed up from behind her shoulder... Poor Perekladin was tormented all night. And even in the morning, the phantom did not go away. He saw it everywhere: in his boots, as he was putting them on; in a saucer of tea; and in his Order of Stanislaus*…

"'And other feelings…'" he thought. "It's true that I've never experienced any feelings. Right now, for instance, I'm going to my chief's house to sign the guest book by way of Christmas greetings… But is that done with feeling?… It's all meaningless… A greeting machine…"

When Perekladin went out into the street and hailed a cab, it seemed to him that instead of a cabbie an exclamation mark came driving up.

When he walked into his chief's antechamber, he saw the same exclamation mark in place of a doorman… And all these things kept speaking to him of rapture, indignation, wrath… The penholder also looked like an exclamation mark. Perekladin picked it up, dipped the pen in the inkwell, and signed: "Collegiate Secretary Yefim Perekladin!!!"

And as he wrote those three exclamation marks, he was rapturous, he was indignant, he was joyous, and he boiled with wrath. "That for you! Take that!" he muttered, bearing down hard on the pen.

The fiery exclamation mark was satisfied, and vanished.

– 1885

The Speech-Maker

ONE FINE MORNING THEY were burying Collegiate Assessor Kirill Ivanovich Vavilonov, who had died from those two diseases so widespread in our country: a venomous wife and alcoholism. As the funeral cortège was proceeding from the church to the cemetery, one of the deceased's colleagues, a certain Poplavsky, got into a cab and rushed to the lodgings of his friend Grigory Petrovich Zapoykin, a young man but already rather popular. Zapoykin, as many of my readers know, possesses a rare talent for making impromptu speeches at weddings, anniversaries and funerals. He can speak at any old time at all: when he's half-awake, half-starving, dead drunk, or feverish. His words flow smoothly and evenly (like water from a drainpipe) and in great abundance. There are far more pathetic terms in his oratorical vocabulary than there are cockroaches in any tavern. He always speaks eloquently and at great length, so that some- times – especially at merchants' weddings – the assistance of the police must be sought in order to stop him.

"I've come to fetch you," began Poplavsky, having found him at home. "Get dressed right now, and let's be on our way. One of the bunch from my office has died, and we're just now seeing him off to the Great Beyond. Some- body has to say a few words of farewell – some kind of rubbish – and we're counting on you, old boy. If somebody unimportant had died, we wouldn't bother you. But this one was a departmental secretary – a pillar of the office, so to speak."

"Oh, the secretary!" Zapoykin yawned. "You mean that drunk?"

"Yes, the drunk. There'll be pancakes and hors d'oeuvres, and you'll get cab fare. Come along, old chap! Give us some kind of fancy Ciceronian claptrap at the graveside, and you'll get a hearty thanks."

Zapoykin readily agreed. He tousled his hair, assumed a melancholy mien, and went out with Poplavsky.

"I knew that secretary friend of yours," he said, as they got into the cab. "He was one of the foxiest old scoundrels you could find anywhere, God rest his soul…"

"Come now, Grisha. You mustn't sling mud at the dead."

"*Aut mortuis nihil bene*,* of course. But he was still a swindler."

The two friends caught up with the funeral procession and joined it. The deceased was being carried along slowly, so that before reaching the cemetery they managed three times to duck into a tavern and grab a quick drink for the repose of his soul.

At the cemetery, the prayer for the dead had already been recited. In obedience to the custom, the deceased's mother-in-law, his wife and his sister-in-law wept copiously. When the coffin was lowered into the grave, his wife even cried out, "Let me in with him!" But she didn't follow her husband into the grave, apparently having bethought herself of his pension.

Zapoykin waited until everything had quieted down. Then he stepped forward, cast a glance over all his listeners, and began: "Can we believe our own eyes and ears? Is it all not just a bad dream – this coffin, these tear-stained faces, this weeping and wailing? Alas, it is not a dream, and our eyes do not deceive us. He who, only a short time ago, looked so hearty, so youthfully fresh and pure; he, whom only a short while ago we watched as, like unto the indefatigable bees, he brought his honey to the communal hive of the national order and harmony; he who… that same one has now become dust – a material mirage. Implacable Death laid its stiffening hand on him at a time when, despite his stooping age, he was still full of the bloom of strength and radiant hopes. An irreplaceable loss! Who can ever take his place? We have many good civil servants, but Prokofy Osipych was unique. To the very bottom of his soul he was dedicated to his honourable duty. He never spared his strength, he never slept at night, he was selfless and incorruptible… How he scorned those who, to the prejudice of the national interest, attempted to bribe him – those who tried by means of seductive creature comforts to lure him into betraying his duty! Yes, before our very eyes Prokofy Osipych distributed his salary among his most needy comrades. And just now, you yourselves have heard the wails of the widows and orphans supported

by his alms. Dedicated to his official duty and
to good works, he partook of no joys in his
lifetime, and even denied himself the hap-
piness of a family life. As you are all aware,
he was a bachelor until the end of his days.
And who will take his place among us as
a comrade? As though it were right now, I
can see his compassionate, clean-shaven face
turned towards us with a kindly smile. As
though it were right now, I can hear his gen-
tle, tender, friendly voice. Peace to thy ashes,
Prokofy Osipych! Rest in peace, noble and
honourable toiler!"

Zapoykin continued, but his listeners had
begun to whisper. They all liked the speech,
and it had wrung a few tears out of them;
but there was a good deal in it that seemed

strange. In the first place, it was incomprehensible why the speaker called the deceased Prokofy Osipych, whereas his name was Kirill Ivanovich. In the second place, everybody knew that the deceased had battled all his life with his wife, to whom he had been married in proper form; hence he could not be called a bachelor. In the third place, he had had a bushy red beard, and had never shaved in all his life, so that it was incomprehensible why the speaker referred to his face as "clean-shaven".

"Prokofy Osipych!" the speech-maker continued. "Your face was unattractive – even ugly. You were gloomy and stern. But we all knew that beneath that visible exterior there beat an honest, friendly heart!"

Soon the listeners began to notice something strange in the speaker himself. He kept staring in one direction, shifted about nervously, and his shoulders began to jerk.

"I say!" he said, looking about him in terror. "*He's alive.*"

"Who's alive?"

"Why, Prokofy Osipych! He's standing over there by the headstone!"

"But *he* wasn't the one that died! It was Kirill Ivanovich!"

"*What?* You yourself told me the secretary had died!"

"Kirill Ivanovich *was* the secretary. It's true that Prokofy Osipych used to be the secretary. But two years ago he was transferred to the second department as head clerk."

"Oh, only the devil can understand you!"

"Why did you stop? Keep on talking – it's getting embarrassing!"

Zapoykin turned towards the grave again, and with all his former eloquence, resumed his interrupted speech. Sure enough, standing there near the headstone was Prokofy Osipych, an old civil servant with a clean-shaven face. He was looking at the speech-maker and frowning angrily.

On the way back from the burial ceremony, the other civil servants asked Zapoykin with a laugh, "What on earth made you do that? You buried a living man."

"That was not good, young man," grumbled Prokofy Osipych. "Your speech may have been all very well for a dead man, but for a live one it was a jeer. For goodness' sake, what were you saying?

'Selfless, incorruptible, never takes bribes.' Why, things like that can be said about a living man only in mockery! And besides, sir, no one asked you to expatiate upon my face! Unattractive and ugly it may well be – but why put my physiognomy on public display? It's insulting, sir!"

– 1886

Who Is to Blame?

My uncle, PYOTR DEMYANYCH, a skinny, bilious collegiate assessor very much resembling a stale smoked salmon with a stick struck through it, was getting ready to go to the high school where he taught Latin, when he noticed that the binding of his grammar book had been nibbled by mice.

"I say there, Praskovya," he said, going into the kitchen and addressing the cook. "How do we happen to have mice around here? For heaven's sake! Yesterday they chewed holes in my top hat, and now they've desecrated my grammar book. The next thing you know, they'll start eating my clothes!"

"What am I supposed to do about it?" answered Praskovya. "I didn't bring them into the house."

"*Something* has to be done! You could get us a cat, couldn't you?"

"We already have one, but what's he good for? And Praskovya pointed to a corner, where a white kitten, thin as a sliver, was curled up asleep beside a twig broom.

"Why isn't he good for anything?" asked Pyotr Demyanych.

"He's still young and stupid. He can't be as much as two months old yet."

"Hm… Then he should be taught. It would be better for him to be learning than just lying there."

Having said that, Pyotr Demyanych sighed a careworn sigh and walked out of the kitchen.

The kitten raised his head lazily, watched him leave, and again closed his eyes.

The kitten was awake, though, and thinking. About what? Being unfamiliar with real life, and having no store of impressions, he could think only instinctually, and envision life only according to those notions he had inherited, together with his flesh and blood, from his tiger ancestors. (*Vide* Darwin.) His thoughts were on the order of daydreams. His feline imagination pictured something like the Arabian desert, across which moved shadows very much resembling Praskovya, the stove, the broom. Among the shadows there suddenly appeared a saucer of milk. The saucer grew paws, and began to move and manifest an inclination to flee. The kitten pounced and, in a swoon of bloodthirsty voluptuousness, sank his claws into it… When the saucer had vanished into the mist, a piece of meat appeared, dropped by Praskovya. With a cowardly squeak, the meat started to run away; but the kitten pounced, and sank his claws into it… Each one of the young daydreamer's visions had as its starting point pounces, claws and teeth…

The soul of another is a mystery, and a cat's soul even more so. Nonetheless, just how close the foregoing images are to the truth is evident from the following incident. Under the spell of his daydreams, the kitten suddenly gave a start, looked with glittering eyes at Praskovya and, his fur bristling, pounced, sinking his claws into the hem of her skirt. Obviously, he was a born mouser, fully worthy of his bloodthirsty ancestors. Fate had intended him to be the terror of cellars, pantries and granaries. And had it not been for education… But let us not get ahead of the story.

On his way home from the school, Pyotr Demyanych went into a sundries shop and bought a mousetrap for fifteen kopecks. After dinner he put a piece of chopped meat on the hook and placed the trap under the sofa, where there was a pile of students' assignment papers that Praskovya used for household purposes. Exactly at six o'clock in the evening, when the venerable Latinist was sitting at his desk and correcting papers, a sudden *clunk!* came from under the sofa – so loud that my uncle started and dropped his pen. Without delay, he went to the sofa and retrieved the trap. A neat little mouse about the size of a thimble was sniffing the wire of the cage and trembling with fright.

"Aha!" muttered Pyotr Demyanych. And he glared so balefully at the mouse that you'd have thought he was about to give him an "F". "You're caught, you vile creature! Just you wait! I'll show you how to eat grammar books!"

Having had his fill of glaring at his victim, Pyotr Demyanych put the mousetrap on the floor and shouted, "Praskovya! I've caught a mouse! Bring the kitten here!"

"R-r-right away!" Praskovya called back. And a moment later she came in, holding in her arms the descendant of tigers.

"Fine!" muttered Pyotr Demyanych, rubbing his hands. "We're going to teach him… Put

him down by the mousetrap… That's it… Let
him smell it and look at it. That's the way…"

The kitten looked with astonishment at my
uncle, then at his armchair; sniffed the mousetrap with a baffled air; and then – no doubt
having been frightened by the bright lamplight
and all the attention being paid to him – took
off in terror towards the door.

"Stop!" shouted my uncle, seizing him by the
tail. "Stop, you scoundrel! You've been frightened by a *mouse*, you idiot! Look: it's a mouse.
Come, look! Well? *Look*, I tell you!"

Pyotr Demyanych grabbed the kitten by the
scruff of the neck and shoved his nose against
the mousetrap.

"Look, you little bastard! Pick him up,
Praskovya, and hold him… Hold him against

the door of the trap… When I let the mouse out, you let him go at the same time, understand? Let him go at exactly the same time. All right?"

My uncle assumed a conspiratorial expression and raised the door… The mouse emerged hesitantly, sniffed the air, and then darted under the sofa. The liberated kitten hoisted his tail in the air, and ran under the desk.

"It got away! It got away!" shouted Pyotr Demyanych, making a ferocious face. "Where is he, the villain? Under the desk? Just you wait…"

My uncle dragged the kitten out from under the desk and shook him in the air…

"You scum!" he muttered, pulling him by the ear. "Take that! And that! Will you ever flunk like that again? You s-s-scum!"

The next day, Praskovya once again heard the shout: "Praskovya, I've caught a mouse! Bring the kitten here!"

After his humiliation of the day before, the kitten had gone to hide under the stove, and had not come out all night. When Praskovya had dragged him out and, carrying him by the scruff of the neck into the study, had deposited him in front of the mousetrap, he trembled all over and meowed plaintively.

"All right," Pyotr Demyanych commanded. "Let him get the lay of the land first. Let him look and sniff. Look and learn, you! Stop, damn you!" he shouted, noticing that the kitten was backing away from the mousetrap. "I'll thrash you! Hold on to him by the ear. That's it... Now put him down in front of the door."

My uncle slowly raised the door... The mouse whisked right under the kitten's nose, ricocheted off Praskovya's arm, and ran under the bookcase. The kitten, meanwhile, sensing that he was at liberty, made a desperate leap and hid under the sofa.

"He's let another mouse go!" bellowed Pyotr Demyanych. "Do you call that a cat? He's an abomination! Just plain trash! He needs to be thrashed – thrashed right in front of the mousetrap!"

When the third mouse was caught, the kitten trembled all over at the sight of the mouse-trap and its tenant, and scratched Praskovya's hand... After the fourth mouse, my uncle lost all self-control and gave the kitten a kick. "Get rid of this nasty thing!" he said. "I want him out of the house today! Just dump him somewhere. He isn't worth a tinker's damn!"

A year went by. The thin, sickly kitten developed into a solid, sagacious tomcat. One night he was prowling through the backyards on his way to a lovers' tryst. He was already near his destination when suddenly he heard a rustling sound, and then saw a mouse scampering from the horse trough towards the stables... Our hero bristled, arched his back, began to hiss and, shaking all over, pusillanimously took to flight.

Alas! Sometimes I feel that I'm in the ludicrous position of the fleeing tomcat. Like the kitten, I had the honour in my time of studying Latin with my uncle. Today, whenever I chance to see some work of classical antiquity, instead of going into wild raptures about it

I begin to recall the *ut consecutivum*,* the irregular verbs, the sallow-grey face of my uncle, and the ablative absolute... I go pale, my hair stands on end, and like the tomcat, I take off in ignominious flight.

– 1886

A Defenceless Creature

No MATTER HOW BAD his attack of gout had been during the night, nor how raw it left his nerves, Kistunov always went to his office in the morning and began promptly to receive the petitioners and clients of the bank. But he looked enfeebled and weary, and spoke in a scarcely audible voice, like a dying man.

"What can I do for you?" he said (one such morning) to a lady petitioner in an antediluvian coat who from the rear resembled a large dung beetle.

"Just consider, Your Excellency!" she began very rapidly. "My husband, Collegiate Assessor Shchukin, was sick for five months. And while he was lying in bed – if you will pardon the expression – and taking treatments, Your Excellency, he was retired for no reason at all. And when I went to get his pay, understand, they deducted twenty-four roubles and thirty-six kopecks from it. 'For what?' I asked them. 'Because,' said they, 'he borrowed from the employees' fund, and other clerks cosigned for him.' How could that be? As if he could borrow any money without my approval! That's impossible, Your Excellency! And why, I ask you? I'm a poor woman. I barely make a living by taking in boarders. I'm weak and defenceless… I take insults from everybody, and don't hear a kind word from anybody…"

The lady began to blink and reached into her coat pocket for her handkerchief. Kistunov took her petition and began to read it. "Excuse me," he said with a shrug, "but what's this all about? I simply don't understand. It is obvious, madam, that you have come to the wrong place. Actually, your petition has nothing whatsoever to do with us. You'll have to go to the agency where your husband was employed."

"What do you mean, my good sir? I've been to five places already," said Madame Shchukina, "and they wouldn't even look at my petition. I was about ready to lose my mind. But my son-in-law, Boris Matveich — my thanks to him, and may God give him health! — suggested that I come to see you. '*Mamasha*,'* he said, 'go to see Mr Kistunov. He's a man of influence. He can do everything for you!... Help me, Your Excellency!"

"I'm sorry, madam, but there's nothing at all we can do for you. You must try to understand. Your husband, so far as I can make out, was an employee of the Department of Military Medicine. But our institution is completely private and commercial. We run a bank. Surely you can understand *that* much!"

Kistunov shrugged again, and turned to a gentleman in military uniform with a swollen cheek.

"Your Excellency!" Madame Shchukina cried out plaintively. "I have a doctor's certificate to prove that my husband was sick. Here it is. Please look at it!"

"Wonderful!" Kistunov said irritably. "I quite believe you. But I must repeat: this has nothing to do with us. It's strange – even ridiculous! Can it be possible that your husband doesn't know what agency you should go to?"

"He doesn't know anything, Your Excellency. He just kept saying, 'It's none of your business! Get out of here!' That's all he said… But then, whose business is it? After all, it's my back that's bearing the burden. Mine!"

Kistunov once again turned to Madame Shchukina and began explaining the difference between the Department of Military Medicine and a private bank. She listened to him attentively, nodded her head in agreement, and then said, "Yes, yes. I understand, sir. In that case, Your Excellency, have them pay me only fifteen roubles. I don't have to have all of it right away."

"*Oof!*" sighed Kistunov, throwing his head back. "There's just no way to get it into your head! If you'd just realize that to come to us with this kind of claim is as strange as, let us say, trying to get a divorce at a drugstore or an assay office. You may have some money coming to you, but what do we have to do with it?"

"Your Excellency, I'll be eternally grateful to you! Have pity on me, an orphan!" Madame Shchukina implored him tearfully. "I'm a weak, defenceless woman... I'm exhausted to the point of death. I'm suing my boarders and fussing over my husband and running this way and that taking care of the household, and on top of it all I'm fasting and my son-in-law is out of work... It's a wonder I can still eat and drink. I can hardly stand on my own two feet... I didn't get a wink of sleep last night."

Kistunov's heart began to flutter. With an expression of acute suffering, and with his hand on his heart, he once again began to explain to Madame Shchukina. But his voice failed him…

"You must excuse me," he said, with a wave of the hand, "but I can't speak to you any longer. My head is spinning. You are holding us up, and wasting your own time. *Oof!* Alexei Nikolaich," he said, turning to one of his assistants, "please explain things to Madame Shchukina."

When he had dealt with all his other petitioners, Kistunov returned to his private office and signed some dozen documents; meantime, Alexei Nikolaich was still trying to cope with Madame Shchukina. Sitting in his office, Kistunov listened for a long time to the two voices: the monotonous, restrained bass of Alexei

Nikolaich, and the plaintive, whining voice of Madame Shchukina.

"I'm a weak, defenceless woman," Madame Shchukina was saying, "a sick woman. And if the truth be told, there's not a healthy bone in my body. I can hardly stand on my own two feet, and I don't have any more appetite. I drank some coffee this morning, but I didn't enjoy it at all."

Alexei Nikolaich, for his part, went on explaining the difference among agencies, and the complex system of routing documents. But he soon wore out, and a bookkeeper replaced him.

"An amazingly headstrong woman!" Kistunov exclaimed, nervously twisting his fingers and repeatedly going to the water decanter.

"She's an idiot! A nitwit! She wore me clear out, and now she's wearing them out, damn her! *Oof!* My heart is fluttering!"

Half an hour later he rang, and Alexei Nikolaich came in.

"How is it going?" Kistunov asked wearily.

"Can't get a thing into her head, Pyotr Alexandrych! I'm simply exhausted. We're at sixes and sevens."

"I just can't stand the sound of her voice... I'm ill... I can't bear it."

"Call the doorman, Pyotr Alexandrych, and tell him to get her out of here."

"Oh, no!" exclaimed Kistunov in alarm. "She'd start screaming. There are lots of apartments in this building, and the Lord only knows what people might think we were up to... Just try once more to explain it to her somehow, my boy."

A minute later the low hum of Alexei Nikola-ich's voice could again be heard. A quarter of an hour later, it was replaced by the strong tenor of the bookkeeper.

"R-r-remarkably vile!" exclaimed Kistunov in exasperation, his shoulders jerking convulsively. "As stupid as they come, damn her! It feels like my gout is kicking up again… And my headache…"

In the next office, Alexei Nikolaich, having finally reached breaking point, rapped his finger on his desk and then against his forehead. "In short," he said, "what you have on your shoulders is not a head but a block of—"

"Well, I must say!" exclaimed the lady, insulted. "Go beat on your own wife, you… you nothing! Don't be so free with your hands!"

Giving her a wrathful look, enraged enough to swallow her, Alexei Nikolaich said in a quiet, smothered voice: "Get out!"

"*W-w-what?*" Madame Shchukina suddenly screeched. "How dare you? I'm a weak woman – defenceless. I won't allow it! My husband is a collegiate assessor. You pipsqueak! I'll go to Dmitry Karlych, the lawyer, and you'll have no position left! I've had three boarders sentenced! You'll fall on your knees to me for those impudent words! I'll go to see your general! Your Excellency! Your Excellency!"

"Get out of here, you plague!" hissed Alexei Nikolaich.

Kistunov opened the door and looked into the office. "What is it?' he asked in a querulous voice.

Madame Shchukina, red as a lobster, was standing in the middle of the room and, her eyes rolling, was poking her fingers into the air. Some bank clerks were standing along the sides of the room and, also red, and obviously embarrassed, were looking at one another in confusion.

Madame Shchukina threw herself on Kistunov. "Your Excellency! That one there – that very one – that one" (she pointed to Alexei Nikolaich) "rapped with his finger on his forehead, and then on the desk... You ordered him to look into my case, but he is mocking me! I'm a weak woman, defenceless... My husband is a collegiate assessor. And I myself am a major's daughter!"

"All right, madam," Kistunov sighed. "I'll take care of it. I'll take steps... Just go on out, now. Later..."

"But when will I get it, Your Excellency? I need the money now!"

With a trembling hand, Kistunov wiped his brow, sighed, and once again began to explain. "Madam, I have already told you: this is a bank – a private commercial establishment. So what do you want of us? And please *do* get it through your head that you're bothering us!"

Shchukina listened to him and sighed. "All right, all right," she agreed. "But you, Your Excellency, do me the favour – I'll be eternally grateful to you. Be my benefactor and protect me. If the doctor's certificate isn't enough, I can get one from the police station. Make them pay me my money!"

Kistunov's head began to swim. He blew out all the air that was in his lungs, and sat down on a chair, exhausted. "How much do you want?" he asked in a weak voice.

"Twenty-four roubles and thirty-six kopecks."

Kistunov reached into his pocket and took out a wallet, from which he took a twenty-five-rouble bill and gave it to the old lady. "Take this, and leave!"

She wrapped the money up in a little handkerchief, hid it, and, crinkling her face into a saccharine, delicate, even coquettish smile, asked: "Your Excellency, can't my husband return to his job?"

"I'm leaving… I'm sick," said Kistunov in a faint voice. "My heart is fluttering badly."

When he left, Alexei Nikolaich sent Nikita for cherry-laurel drops; and all of them, having taken twenty drops apiece, went back to work. But Madame Shchukina sat in the waiting room for another two hours, talking with the doorman and waiting for Kistunov to return.

She was back again the next day.

– 1887

Notes

p. 5, *The Chimes of Normandy*: An operetta by the French composer Robert Planquette (1848–1903), known in French as *Les Cloches de Corneville*. It was first performed in 1877.

p. 22, *batyushka*: "Dear friend" (Russian).

p. 36, *knucklebones*: Another name for jacks, a game involving the tossing and catching of small pebbles.

p. 57, *dushenka*: "Darling" (Russian).

p. 60, *Order of Stanislaus*: An imperial medal, originally Polish but part of the Russian awards system after 1832.

p. 68, *Aut mortuis nihil bene*: More usually *De*

mortuis aut nihil aut bene: "Speak well of the dead or not at all" (Latin).

p. 90, *ut consecutivum*: A Latin syntactical construction involving the usage of *ut* ("that"; "so that") to introduce a "consecutive clause", e.g. *tam strene laborabat ut defessus esset*: "he was working so hard that he was tired".

p. 95, *Mamasha*: "Mama" (Russian).

Biographical Note

Anton Pavlovich Chekhov was born on 29th January 1860 (New Style) in Taganrog, a port on the Sea of Azov in southern Russia, to Pavel Yegorovich Chekhov, a former serf, and Yevgenia Yakovlevna. He began his education at a school for the descendants of Greek merchants (then held in higher regard than its Russian alternatives), but soon transferred to the Taganrog gymnasium, where he received the remainder of his schooling. In 1875 Chekhov's father was declared bankrupt and fled to Moscow, leaving

his family to face the creditors; soon after, however, the remainder of the family followed him
to Moscow with the exception of the young
Anton, who remained behind with the new
owner of the family's estate.

Having assiduously applied himself to his
studies, Chekhov passed the leaving exams with
distinction in June 1879 and moved to Moscow
the following autumn to study medicine at Moscow University. During this period, Chekhov
worked to support his family, then still living in
a one-room apartment in Moscow, by writing a
number of short sketches for satirical magazines
and journals. By 1880, more than one hundred
of these had been printed under a series of pseu-
donyms (the most renowned being "Antosha
Chekhonte"). Later in 1880, becoming more

confident in his abilities, Chekhov sent a draft of his first play to the Maly Theatre. The draft was rejected, and Chekhov lay the work aside; it was seen in print for the first time only in 1920, published under the title *Platonov*. Undeterred, however, Chekhov continued to write short stories and sketches for various Moscow journals, and in 1882 he became a regular contributor to the St Petersburg journal *Oskolki* ("Splinters"), providing sketches on Moscow life for its readers.

Chekhov graduated from Moscow University in June 1884 and began work as a medical practitioner while still continuing to write, something he would do throughout the entirety of his working life. By 1885 Chekhov had gained considerable notoriety and was invited to St

Petersburg by the editor of the *St Petersburg Journal*. During this visit, Chekhov became acquainted with the press mogul and editor of *Novoye Vremya* (*New Times*), Alexei Suvorin, who asked Chekhov to contribute to the journal, agreeing to pay him sums of money considerably greater than he had ever received before for his writing. Although the initial works were still published pseudonymously, leading writers of the day were successful in persuading Chekhov now to publish under his own name. In 1887, Suvorin published a collection of sixteen of Chekhov's short stories with the collective title *In the Twilight*, for which Chekhov was later to be awarded the Pushkin Prize.

In 1889, having seen the success of his play *Ivanov* and the failure of *The Wood Demon* (later to be reworked as *Uncle Vanya*), Chekhov embarked upon the arduous journey to Sakhalin to document the conditions of the inhabitants of the island. The expedition lasted until October 1890, upon which he returned to Moscow, and later moved with his family to an estate at Melikhovo, some forty miles south of Moscow.

Returning to the theatre, Chekhov's *The Seagull* was premiered at the Alexandinsky Theatre in St Petersburg in October 1896. The performance was a complete failure, which resulted in jeering and laughter from the audience, followed by a number of vicious reviews in the press. However, despite its inauspicious beginnings, *The Seagull* remained in the repertory and fared considerably better in later

productions, particularly as a result of the renowned Nerimovich-Danchenko and Stanislavsky production at the Moscow Art Theatre
in 1898 (at the rehearsals for which he would
meet his future wife, Olga Knipper).

Having first displayed signs of tuberculosis
in 1884, Chekhov's health had deteriorated
so much that by the winter of 1898–99 he
relocated to Yalta on the Black Sea. From
here, he continued his relationship with Olga
Knipper, mainly through written correspond-
ence, and they eventually married on 25th May
1901. It was during this period that Chekhov
penned some of his most famous short stories,
including *The Lady with the Little Dog*, and
his play *The Three Sisters* (premiered on 31st
January 1901).

Chekhov's last great work *The Cherry Orchard* (begun in early 1902) was premiered on 17th January 1904 in a production by Nerimovich-Danchenko and Stanislavsky. By May of the same year, however, Chekhov was terminally ill with tuberculosis, and on 5th July 1904 he died at the German spa resort of Badenweiler.